ALTERNATIVE TREATMENTS TO TBI:

What should you do for Brain Injury Recovery immediately?

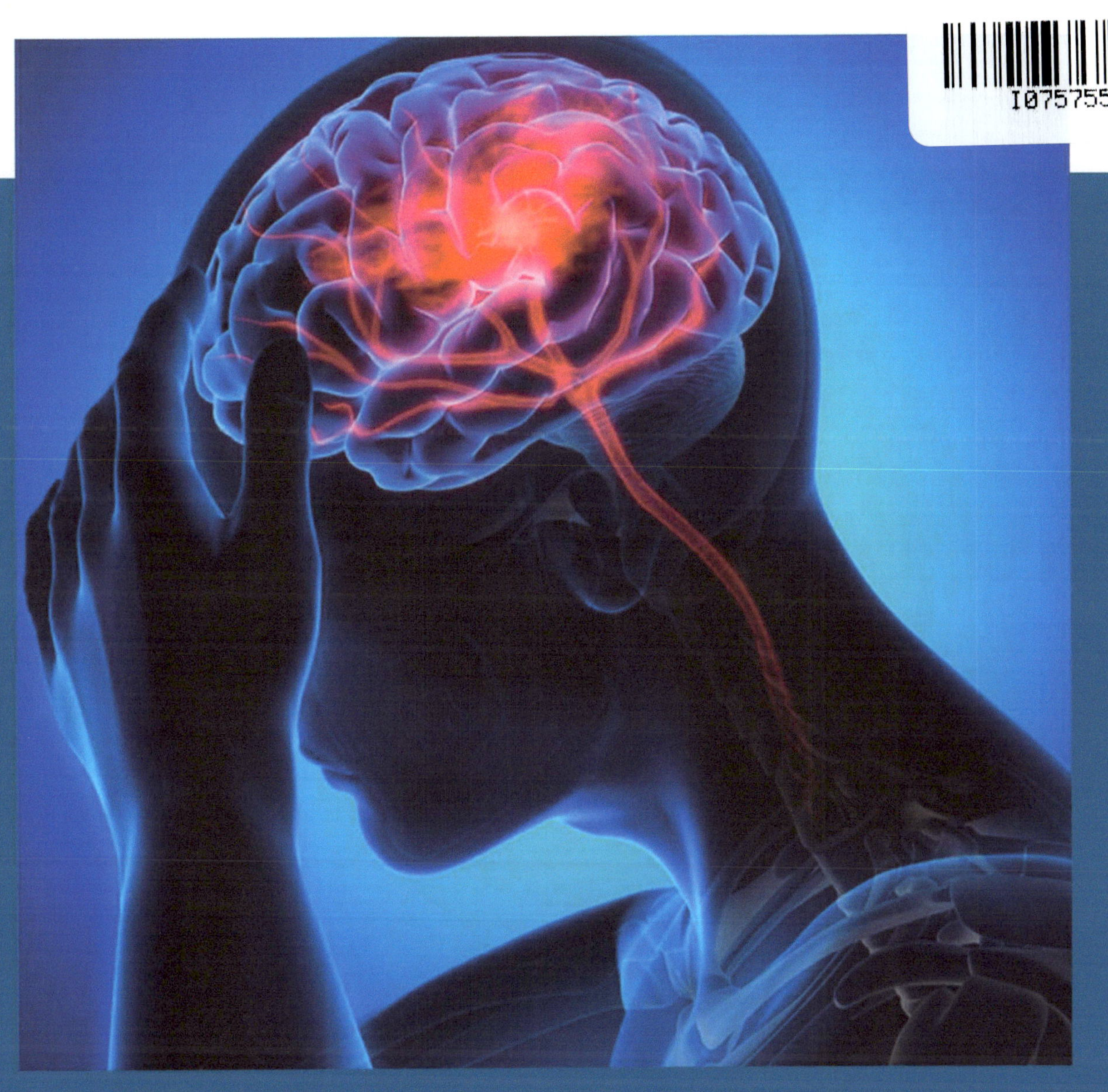

Dr. John W Jung

DEDICATION

This book is dedicated to the late great   George McAndrews JD, whose 15-year legal battle secured the Chiropractic Profession's ability to stand side by side with its Medical colleagues.....

TABLE OF CONTENTS

INTRODUCTION

With more than 50 million people per year and a leading cause of death and disability, traumatic brain injury (TBI) brings a substantial social and economic burden worldwide (1). There are two distinct subtypes of TBI: one is focal brain injury (FBI), which is caused by the brain hitting against the cranium; the other is diffuse axonal injury (DAI) (2), which results from a rotational motion that leads to brain stretching and tearing. TBI is a complex event that refers to any insult to the brain, resulting in primary (direct) mechanic injury and secondary (indirect) insult to the brain parenchyma (3). It remains challenging to fully reveal the pathologically heterogeneity following TBI as it is linked to excitotoxicity, neuroinflammation and cytokine damage, and oxidative damage (4).

- As of 2019, there were **no objective measures** for traumatic brain injury (TBI); current diagnosis involves exams, surveys, and imaging.

- Imaging, such as **CT scans**, can miss TBI early on.

- More advanced imaging, such as **Diffusion Tensor Imaging (DTI)**, may take several months post-injury to show a TBI.

- There are **39.5 million personal injury accidents** requiring medical attention each year.

- Annually, **2.5 million TBI cases** are diagnosed from hospital visits, with another 56% being missed during visits, bringing the total yearly TBI cases to over **5 million**.

This information is based on the "Evaluation of the Disability Determination Process for Traumatic Brain Injury in Veterans."National Academies of Sciences, Engineering, and Medicine; Health and Medicine Division; Board on Health Care Services; Committee on the Review of the Department of Veterans Affairs Examinations for Traumatic Brain Injury.

Washington (DC): National Academies Press (US); 2019 Apr 10.

This is what the doctors tell you when you leave the emergency room with TBI Stroke or Concussion: "Lifestyle Considerations for TBI Recovery"

"Certain lifestyle modifications can support TBI recovery. These include:

- Getting adequate rest and sleep

- Following a balanced diet rich in nutrients.

- Engaging in regular physical activity (as recommended by healthcare providers)

- Practicing stress-reduction techniques such as meditation and deep breathing exercises."

- That's it, you're potentially screwed, since 1 in 3 don't fully recover.

The journey of recovery from such injuries can be challenging, but THERE ARE Dozens of remedies that can aid in the healing process.

In this book, we explore various medicines, herbs and amino acids known to cross the blood-brain barrier and support the recovery of individuals suffering from TBI and concussions. We will also speak of the recent testing that can be done to confirm and predict outcomes with treatment.

You're thinking "Come on now, natural stuff instead of hard-core medicine?"

As an example, I cite a case from 2006.

Omega-3's potential for helping with brain injury was first investigated in the Sago mine collapse in 2006. Randy McCloy was the only survivor of the collapse.

When the rescuers found him in the rubble, he had brain, heart, liver and kidney failure. He was barely clinging to life. After he was transported to West Virginia School of Medicine, the hospital neurosurgeons tube-feed him very large doses of fish oil. Randy has since made a remarkable recovery.

"I certainly think it played a big role," said Dr. Julian Bailes, then Chair of the Department of Neurosurgery. "How can he rebuild his brain, if he doesn't have the substrate to do it?"

Dr. Barry Sears of 'Zone Diet' fame was a consultant for Randy's treatment and has been at the forefront of this new therapy.

5 More info from Pub Med. Concussions, Traumatic Brain Injury, and the Innovative Use of Omega-3s DOI: 10.1080/07315724.2016.1150796

UNDERSTANDING TRAUMATIC BRAIN INJURY AND CONCUSSIONS

Before delving into the specifics of herbs and amino acids, it's crucial to understand the nature of traumatic brain injury and concussions. TBI occurs when an external force injures the brain. Concussions, a milder form of TBI, typically result from a blow or jolt to the head. Symptoms may range from mild to severe and can include headaches, dizziness, memory problems, and mood changes.

The Blood-Brain Barrier and Its Significance

The blood-brain barrier (BBB) is a highly selective membrane that separates the circulating blood from the brain's extracellular fluid. It plays a vital role in protecting the brain from harmful substances while allowing essential nutrients to pass through. Substances that can cross the BBB hold immense potential in treating brain-related conditions, including TBI and concussions.

Accumulating evidence suggests that chronic post-stroke **intracerebral microglial** activation and neuroinflammation, mediated by pathologic levels of tumor necrosis factor, constitute new therapeutic targets that **may persist for years after a stroke.**

TBI pathophysiology can be subdivided into two stages:

The primary injury causes direct mechanical damage of blood vessels and parenchymal cells at the lesion site, subsequent secondary injury develops over a period from minutes to weeks and, potentially, months or years.

Secondary pathology is characterized by an early increase in glutamate and reactive oxygen species, as well as the occurrence of mitochondrial dysfunction and increased expression of cytokines and chemokines. **IKK2/NF-κB signaling protects neurons after traumatic brain injury** . 2018 Jan 5;32(4):1916–1932. doi: 10.1096/fj.201700826R

Stimulus: The pathway is typically activated by various stimuli, such as pro-inflammatory cytokines (e.g., **TNF-alpha (Tumor Necrosis Factor-alpha)**), bacterial or viral infections, oxidative stress, and other stress signals. Once it starts, it really never slows down. But there are natural ways that have been shown to help.

Summary: Recovering from traumatic brain injury and concussions requires a comprehensive approach that addresses both physical and cognitive aspects of healing. Herbs and amino acids that can cross the blood-brain barrier offer promising avenues for supporting brain health and function during the recovery process. By integrating these natural remedies with lifestyle modifications and professional medical guidance, individuals can optimize their chances of a full and timely recovery.

Additional References

Kennedy, D. O. (2000). Herbal extracts and phytochemicals: Plant secondary metabolites and the enhancement of human brain function. Advances in Nutrition Research, 10(Supplement C), 47–73.

Stough, C., Downey, L. A., Lloyd, J., Silber, B., Redman, S., Hutchison, C., & Wesnes, K. (2008). Examining the cognitive effects of a special extract of Bacopa monniera (CDRI 08: KeenMind): A review of ten years of research at Swinburne University. Journal of Pharmacy & Pharmaceutical Sciences, 11(3), 325–354.

Nobre, A. C., Rao, A., & Owen, G. N. (2008). L-theanine, a natural constituent in tea, and its effect on mental state. Asia Pacific Journal of Clinical Nutrition, 17(S1), 167–168.

Montgomery, S. A., & Thal, L. J. (1991). Acetyl-L-carnitine in the treatment of Alzheimer's disease. Acta Neurologica Scandinavica, 84(1), 8–11.

INTEGRATING SCAT-5 EVALUATION IN TBI RECOVERY

Traumatic brain injuries (TBIs) and concussions require careful assessment to guide treatment and monitor progress. The Sports Concussion Assessment Tool 5 (SCAT-5) from 2016 is a standardized tool used by healthcare professionals to evaluate individuals suspected of sustaining a concussion. Integrating SCAT-5 evaluation into the recovery process can provide valuable insights into the severity of the injury and aid in developing tailored treatment plans.

SCAT-5 has several components helping to assess various aspects of cognitive function, balance, and symptom severity. These components include:

Symptom Evaluation: Patients are asked to report any symptoms they may be experiencing, such as headaches, dizziness, or memory problems. The severity and duration of these symptoms are recorded to track progress over time.

Cognitive Assessment: This section evaluates cognitive function through tasks such as memory recall, concentration, and reaction time. Healthcare professionals may use standardized tests such as the Standardized Assessment of Concussion (SAC) to assess cognitive performance.

Balance Assessment: Balance impairment is common following a concussion. SCAT-5 includes tests such as the modified Balance Error Scoring System (mBESS) to assess balance and postural stability.

Coordination Evaluation: Coordination and motor function may be affected by a TBI, including tests such as the tandem gait test to assess coordination and motor skills.

Role of SCAT-5 in TBI Recovery

Integrating SCAT-5 evaluation into the TBI recovery process offers several benefits:

Objective Assessment: SCAT-5 provides a standardized framework for evaluating TBI symptoms and cognitive function. This allows healthcare professionals to objectively assess the severity of the injury and track progress over time.

Tailored Treatment Planning: By identifying specific areas of impairment using SCAT-5, healthcare professionals can develop personalized treatment plans tailored to the individual's needs. For example, patients with cognitive deficits may benefit from cognitive rehabilitation therapy, while those with balance impairments may require vestibular rehabilitation.

Monitoring Progress: Regular administration of SCAT-5 allows healthcare professionals to monitor the patient's progress throughout the recovery process. Changes in symptom severity, cognitive function, and balance can be tracked over time, guiding adjustments to the treatment plan as needed.

Return-to-Play Decision Making: For individuals involved in sports or physical activities, SCAT-5 can help inform return-to-play decisions. By assessing cognitive function, balance, and symptom severity, healthcare professionals can determine when it is safe for an individual to resume activity without risking further injury.

SCAT-5 evaluation plays a crucial role in the management of TBIs and concussions, providing healthcare professionals with valuable information to guide treatment and monitor progress. By integrating SCAT-5 assessment into the recovery process, individuals can receive personalized care tailored to their specific needs, ultimately optimizing outcomes and facilitating a safe return to normal activities.

References

Echemendia, R. J., Meeuwisse, W., McCrory, P., Davis, G. A., Putukian, M., Leddy, J., ... & Turner, M. (2017). The Sport Concussion Assessment Tool 5th Edition (SCAT5): Background and rationale. British Journal of Sports Medicine, 51(11), 848-850.

Giza, C. C., Kutcher, J. S., Ashwal, S., Barth, J., Getchius, T. S. D., Gioia, G. A., ... & Zafonte, R. (2013). Summary of evidence-based guideline update: Evaluation and management of concussion in sports: Report of the Guideline Development Subcommittee of the American Academy of Neurology. Neurology, 80(24), 2250-2257.

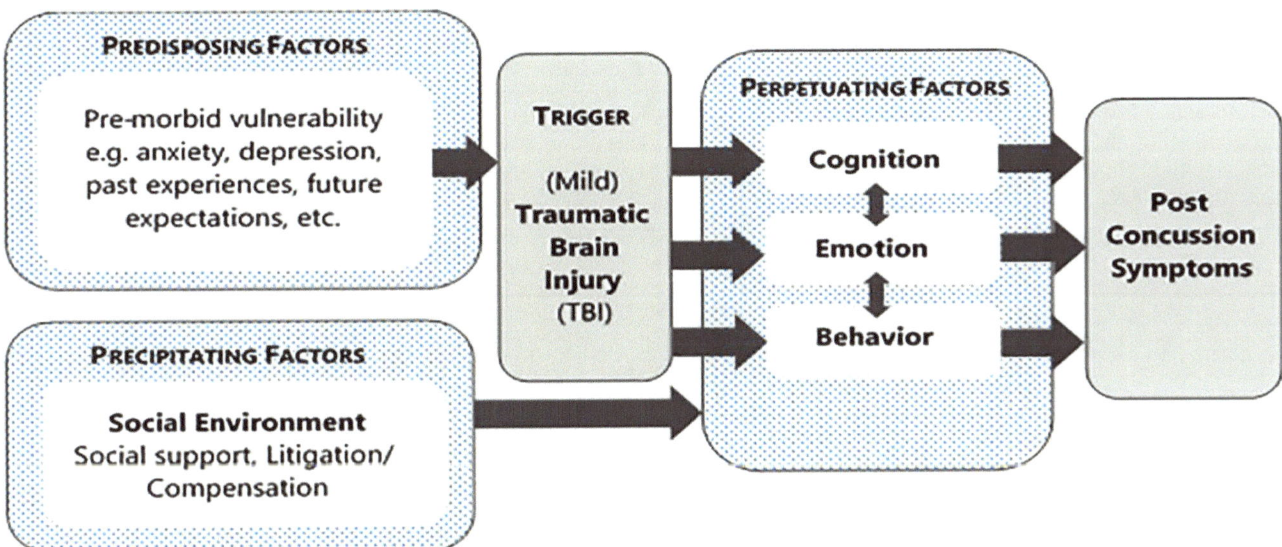

Since most people recover from their TBI within weeks to months after the injury, post-concussion symptoms might easily be overlooked, since these residual complaints may be deferred. Furthermore, imaging techniques often do not show any structural brain damage in this population. Still, one in three TBI patients will not be able to do any work and act within six months after the event's level similar to that before the accident. As a consequence, TBI is associated with substantial ongoing disability and distress for patients, and high health care costs.

A possible tool for (early) identification to timely guide clinical management to post-concussion symptoms after TBI, is the Rivermead Post Concussion Syndrome Questionnaire (RPQ). The RPQ is a validated measurement instrument to survey post-concussion symptoms, relying on self-report as to the presence and severity of 16 symptoms. PLOSONE| https://doi.org/10.1371/journal.pone.0210138October24,2019

Most of the individuals who experience traumatic brain injury (TBI) develop neuropsychiatric and cognitive complications that negatively affect recovery and health span. Activation of multiple inflammatory pathways persists after TBI, ... One outcome of TBI is microglial priming and subsequent hyper-reactivity to secondary stressors, injuries, or immune challenges... microglia priming with aging contributes to exaggerated glial responses to TBI. One prominent inflammatory pathway, interferon (IFN) signaling, is increased after TBI and may contribute to microglial priming and subsequent reactivity. Trends Neurosci. 2023 Nov;46(11):926–940. doi: 10.1016/j.tins.2023.08.008

DEFINITION OF AXONAL SHEARING

Axonal shearing, also known as diffuse axonal injury (DAI), is a type of traumatic brain injury (TBI) that occurs when the brain rapidly shifts inside the skull as an injury is occurring. This sudden movement can cause the axons, the long thread-like part of a nerve cell along which impulses are conducted, to stretch or tear. Axonal shearing disrupts the brain's communication system, leading to widespread damage across multiple brain regions. Axonal shearing is often the result of severe acceleration or deceleration forces, such as those experienced in high-speed motor vehicle accidents, falls, or sports injuries. This type of injury can be particularly devastating because it impacts a large area of the brain, rather than being confined to a specific region.

Diagnosis of Axonal Shearing with Advanced Neuroimaging Diagnosing axonal shearing can be challenging due to the diffuse nature of the injury and the microscopic scale of the axonal damage. However, advances in neuroimaging techniques have significantly improved the ability to detect and assess this type of injury.

So how is TBI diagnosed and treated medically now? (Actually, very poorly!)

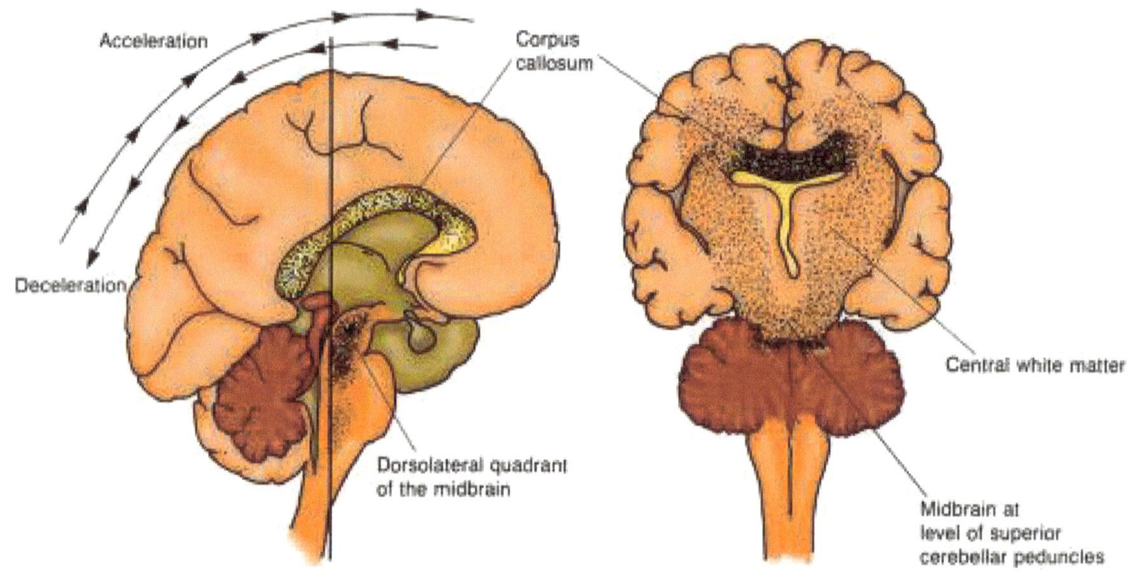

Traditional Imaging Techniques:

1. CT Scans (Computed Tomography): While CT scans are commonly used in the acute setting to identify hemorrhages, fractures, and other gross abnormalities, they are less sensitive in detecting axonal shearing. CT scans might miss the microscopic injuries and subtle changes in brain tissue associated with DAI.

2. MRI (Magnetic Resonance Imaging): Conventional MRI techniques, including T1-weighted, T2-weighted, and FLAIR (Fluid-Attenuated Inversion Recovery) images, offer improved sensitivity over CT scans. MRI can identify brain swelling, small hemorrhages, and other indicators of axonal injury. However, traditional MRI still has limitations in detecting the diffuse and microscopic nature of axonal shearing

Advanced Neuroimaging Techniques:

3. Diffusion Tensor Imaging (DTI): DTI is an advanced form of MRI that measures the diffusion of water molecules along white matter tracts in the brain. This technique is particularly useful for detecting changes in the integrity of axons. In cases of axonal shearing, DTI can reveal disruptions in the white matter pathways, providing critical information about the extent and location of the injury. Studies have shown that DTI can detect abnormalities in the brain even when conventional MRI appears normal.

4. Susceptibility-Weighted Imaging (SWI): SWI is another advanced MRI technique that is highly sensitive to blood products and microhemorrhages. It can detect small, diffuse hemorrhages that are often associated with axonal shearing. The presence of these microhemorrhages can be indicative of the shearing forces that have caused the axonal injury.

5. Functional MRI (fMRI): fMRI measures brain activity by detecting changes in blood flow. Although not typically used for initial diagnosis, fMRI can be valuable in assessing the functional impact of axonal shearing on specific brain regions. This can help in understanding the cognitive and behavioral deficits associated with the injury.

6. Magnetic Resonance Spectroscopy (MRS): MRS provides information about the chemical composition of brain tissue. In cases of axonal shearing, MRS can detect metabolic changes in the brain that are indicative of cellular injury and axonal damage. This technique can complement other imaging methods by providing biochemical evidence of injury.

7. There are even new biomarker blood tests that can determine TBI and post concussion, that will be discussed in further chapters, that most hospitals don't use yet.

References

1. Niogi, S. N., & Mukherjee, P. (2010). Diffusion tensor imaging of mild traumatic brain injury. Journal of Head Trauma Rehabilitation, 25(4), 241–255.

2. Hulkower, M. B., Poliak, D. B., Rosenbaum, S. B., Zimmerman, M. E., & Lipton, M. L. (2013). A decade of DTI in traumatic brain injury: 10 years and 100 articles later. American Journal of Neuroradiology, 34(11), 2064–2074.

3. Haacke, E. M., Mittal, S., Wu, Z., Neelavalli, J., & Cheng, Y. C. (2009). Susceptibility-weighted imaging: technical aspects and clinical applications, part 1. American Journal of Neuroradiology, 30(1), 19–30.

4. Ashwal, S., Holshouser, B., & Tong, K. (2006). Use of advanced neuroimaging techniques in the evaluation of pediatric traumatic brain injury. Developmental Neuroscience, 28(4–5), 309–326.

5. Govind, V., Gold, S., Kaliannan, K., Saigal, G., Falcone, S., & Arheart, K. (2010). Whole-brain proton MR spectroscopy: initial findings in mild traumatic brain injury. American Journal of Neuroradiology, 31(2), 401–408.

So what are other ways TBI is diagnosed currently?

American Congress of Rehabilitation Medicine Diagnostic Criteria for Mild Traumatic Brain Injury:

Mild traumatic brain injury (TBI) is diagnosed when, following a biomechanically plausible mechanism of injury (Criterion

1. One or more of the criteria (i–iii) listed below are met.
    - I. One or more clinical signs (Criterion 2) attributable to brain injury.
    - II. At least 2 acute symptoms (Criterion 3) and at least one clinical or laboratory finding (Criterion 4) attributable to brain injury.
    - III. Neuroimaging evidence of TBI, such as unambiguous trauma–related intracranial abnormalities on computed tomography or structural magnetic resonance imaging (Criterion 5).

Confounding factors do not fully account for the clinical signs (Criterion 2), acute symptoms (Criterion 3), and clinical examination and laboratory findings (Criterion 4) that are necessary for the diagnosis (Criterion 6).

Mild Qualifier: The 'mild' qualifier is not used if any of the injury severity indicators listed below are present. Instead, traumatic brain injury (TBI) is diagnosed (without the 'mild' qualifier)

- i. Loss of consciousness duration greater than 30 minutes.
- ii. After 30 minutes, a Glasgow Coma Scale (GCS) of less than 13.
- iii. Post–traumatic amnesia greater than 24 hours.

Neuroimaging Qualifier: If neuroimaging is abnormal (Criterion 5), the qualifier mild TBI 'with neuroimaging evidence of structural intracranial injury' may be used. When neuroimaging is completed and found to be normal, the qualifier mild TBI 'without neuroimaging evidence of structural intracranial injury' may be used. If neuroimaging is not completed, no qualifier is used.

Concussion: The diagnostic label 'concussion' may be used interchangeably with 'mild TBI' when neuroimaging is normal or not clinically indicated,..

Suspected Mild TBI: A mild TBI is suspected when, following a biomechanically plausible mechanism of injury (Criterion 1), one or more of the3 criteria listed below are met.

- i. At least 2 acute symptoms (Criterion 3) and the person does not meet other criteria sufficient for diagnosing mild TBI
- ii. .ii. At least 2 clinical examination or laboratory findings (Criterion 4) but the person does not meet other criteria for diagnosing mild TBI.
- iii. iii. It is unclear whether signs (Criterion 2), acute symptoms (Criterion 3), and available clinical or laboratory findings (Criterion 4) areaccounted for by confounding factors (ie, it is unclear if Criterion 6 is met).See Box 2for definitions and explanatory notes.1348

  N.D. Silverberg et alwww.archives-pmr.org   [Definitions, Explanatory Notes, and Qualifiers for the American Congress of Rehabilitation Medicine Diagnostic Criteria for Mild Traumatic Brain Injury.]

Criterion 1: Mechanism of Injury Traumatic brain injury (TBI) results from a transfer of mechanical energy to the brain from external forces resulting from the (1) head being struck with an object; (2) head striking a hard object or surface; (3) brain undergoing an acceleration/deceleration movement without direct contact between the head and an object or surface; and/or (4) forces generated from a blast or explosion.

Notes: Criterion 1 can be met by direct observation (in person or video review) or collateral (witness) report of the injury event, review of acute care records, or the person's recount of the injury event during an interview.

Criterion 2: Clinical Signs

The injury event causes an acute physiological disruption of brain function, as manifested by one or more of the clinical signs listed below

i. Loss of consciousness immediately following injury (eg, no protective action taken on falling after impact or lying motionless and unresponsive).

ii. Alteration of mental status immediately following the injury (or upon regaining consciousness), evidenced by reduced responsiveness or inappropriate responses to external stimuli; slowness to respond to questions or instructions; agitated behavior; inability to follow two-part commands; or disorientation to time, place, or situation.

iii. Complete or partial amnesia for events immediately following the injury (or after regaining consciousness). If post-traumatic amnesia cannot be reliably assessed (eg, due to polytrauma or sedating analgesics), retrograde amnesia (ie, a gap in memory for events immediately preceding the injury) can be used as a replacement for this criterion.iv. Other acute neurologic sign(s) (eg, observed motor incoordination upon standing, seizure, or tonic posturing immediately following injury).

Notes: Criterion 2 can be met by direct observation (in person or video review), collateral (witness) report, review of acute care records, or when none of these are available, the person's recount of the injury event.

Criterion 3: Acute Symptoms

The physiological disruption of brain function is manifested by 2or more new or worsened symptoms from the list below

i. Acute subjective alteration in mental status: feeling confused, feeling disoriented, and/or feeling dazed.

ii. Physical symptoms: headache, nausea, dizziness, balance problems, vision problems, sensitivity to light, and/or sensitivity to noise.

iv. Cognitive symptoms: feeling slowed down, "mental fog," difficulty concentrating, and/or memory problems.

iii. Emotional symptoms: uncharacteristic emotional lability and/or irritability. The symptoms may be from one or more categories (ie, experiencing 2 symptoms within a single category is sufficient). Other symptoms may be present, but they should not be counted toward Criterion 3. The onset of acute subjective alteration in mental status occurs immediately following the impact or after regaining consciousness. The onset of other symptoms (physical, cognitive, and emotional) may be delayed by a few hours, but they nearly always appear less than 72 hours from injury.

iv. Notes: Criterion 3 can be met by (1) review of acute care documentation of the injured person's acute symptoms, (2) interviewing the injured person about the first few days following injury; (3) having the injured person complete a self-report rating scale documenting symptoms during the first few days following injury; or (4) collateral observation for an individual who cannot accurately report symptoms due to developmental stage (eg, children under 5 years old) or pre-injury disability.

v.   Criterion 4: Clinical Examination and Laboratory Findings

vi.   The assessment findings listed below can also provide supportive evidence of brain injury.

vii.   Cognitive impairment on acute clinical examination.

viii.   Balance impairment on acute clinical examination.

ix.   Oculomotor impairment or symptom provocation in response to vestibular–oculomotor challenge on acute clinical examination.

x.   Elevated blood biomarker(s) indicative of intracranial injury.

xi.   Notes: Clinical and laboratory tests that meet standards of reliability and diagnostic accuracy should be considered for Criterion 4. Impairment in Criterion 4i–iii is defined as a clinically meaningful discrepancy between post–injury test performance and age–appropriate normative reference data, or where available, pre–injury test performance. The diagnostic sensitivity of most clinical and laboratory tests decreases over the first 72 hours following injury and the rate of sensitivity decline differs between specific tests. Note: this is the old way of thinking.

        a. Criterion 5: Neuroimaging Trauma–related intracranial abnormalities on computed tomography or structural magnetic resonance imaging

xii.   Notes: Neuroimaging is not necessary to diagnose mild TBI. Its primary clinical role is to rule out head and brain injuries that might require neurosurgical or other medical intervention inan acute care setting. When obtained, neuroimaging may reveal intracranial abnormalities indicative of TBI such as contusion(s) or intracranial hemorrhage.

Criterion 6: Not better accounted for by confounding factors Confounding factors, including pre-existing and co–occurring health conditions, have been considered and determined to not fully account for the clinical signs, acute symptoms, and clinical examination and laboratory findings that are necessary for the diagnosis.

Notes: A clinical sign only qualifies for Criterion 2 when it is not better accounted for by acute musculoskeletal pain, psychological trauma, alcohol or substance intoxication, pulmonary or circulatory disruption, syncope prior to fall, or other confounding factors. Symptoms should only be counted toward Criterion 3 when they are not better accounted for by drug, alcohol,or medication use; co–occurring physical injuries (eg, musculoskeletal injury involving the neck or peripheral vestibular dysfunction) or psychological conditions (eg, an acute stress reaction to trauma); pre-existing health conditions; or symptom exaggeration. Criterion 4 findings must not be better accounted for by drug, alcohol, or medication use; co–occurring physical injuries or psychological conditions; pre–existing health conditions; or factors influencing the validity of the symptom reporting or test results.

General Notes: Consideration should be given to cultural and linguistic differences in symptom reporting and test performance. Caution is warranted when applying the diagnostic criteria for mild TBI to young children and individuals with pre–injury cognitive and/or communication impairments. Due to developmental stage (eg, children under 5 years old) or pre–injury disability, an individual may not be able to accurately report symptoms in Criterion 3; thus, this criterion could be met based on proxy report or observation of related behaviors (eg, changes in appetite or behaving out of character). An injured person's behavior should also be interpreted in the context of their developmental stage and pre–injury functioning. Clinical and laboratory test interpretation requires age-appropriate scales and/or cut off scores. Archives of Physical Medicine and Rehabilitation DOI:10.1016/j.apmr.2023.03.036

WHAT ARE THESE BIOMARKERS ABOUT WHICH I AM SO EXCITED?

Biomarkers can be broadly defined as qualitative or quantitative measurements that convey information on the physiopathological state of a subject at a certain time point or disease state. Biomarkers can indicate health, pathology, or response to treatment, including unwanted side effects. When used as outcomes in clinical trials, biomarkers act as surrogates or substitutes for clinically meaningful endpoints. Biomarkers of disease can be diagnostic (the identification of the nature and cause of a condition) or prognostic (predicting the likelihood of a person's survival or outcome of a disease). In addition, genetic biomarkers can be used to quantify the risk of developing a certain disease. In the specific case of traumatic brain injury, surrogate blood biomarkers of imaging can improve the standard of care and reduce the costs of diagnosis. In addition, a prognostic role for biomarkers has been suggested in the case of post-traumatic epilepsy. Given the extensive literature on clinical biomarkers, we will focus herein on biomarkers which are present in peripheral body fluids such as saliva and blood. In particular, blood biomarkers, such as glial fibrillary acidic protein and salivary/blood S100B, will be discussed. Neuropsychiatr Dis Treat. 2018 Nov 8;14:2989–3000. doi: 10.2147/NDT.S125620 SB100

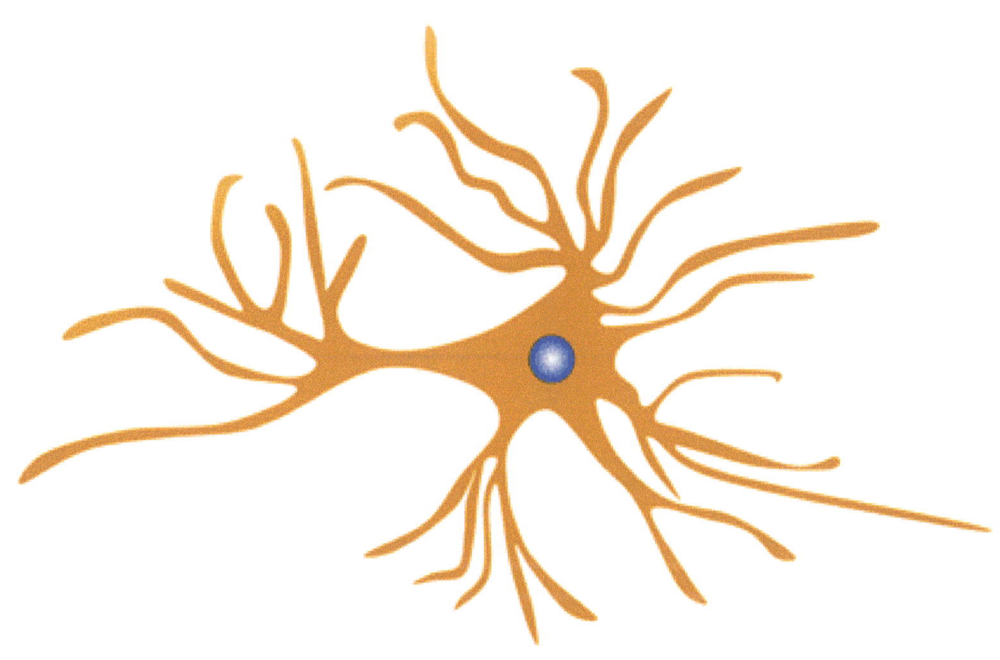

GFAP Glial Injury Marker

Glial Fibrillary Acidic Protein (GFAP) is an astroglia cytoskeletal protein that is exclusive to the central nervous system (CNS). This protein forms networks that provide support and strength to the glial cells. The glial cells nourish and support nerve cells within the brain and spinal cord. If nerve cells are injured glial cells respond by rapidly producing more GFAP. Thus, this protein is released after CNS injury and high levels are associated with neuronal cellular damage. GFAP is a sensitive blood marker for traumatic brain injury (TBI) including mild TBI (mTBI). It is used to aid decisions about whether CT scans of the brain should be performed after TBI .(Values > 6.7 pg/mL are considered positive)

SB 100, also known as **S100B protein**, is a biomarker used in the diagnosis and prognosis of Traumatic Brain Injury (TBI). It is primarily found in astrocytes in the central nervous system and is released into the bloodstream following brain injury. Here are some key points about its use in TBI diagnosis:

1. **Diagnostic Use**: S100B protein levels are measured in serum to help assess the severity of brain injury. Elevated levels can indicate brain damage.

2. **Prognostic Value**: It helps in predicting the clinical outcome and recovery potential of patients with TBI.

3. **Guidelines**: The Scandinavian Neurotrauma Committee (SNC) recommends using S100B as a biomarker for mild TBI. The recommended cut-off value is ≥0.10 μg/L. https://doi.org/10.1186/s13049-022-01062-w

Ubiquitin C-terminal hydrolase-L1 (UCH-L1) is a cytoplasmic protein enzyme found in nerve cells throughout the brain. UCH-L1breaks down damaged and unneeded proteins in nerve cells. Injured nerve cells release UCH-L1 into the blood. Hence, elevated UCH-L1 is a post TBI marker of injury. It is used to aid decisions about whether CT scans of the brain should be performed after TBI.

UCH-L1 protein in bodily fluids, such as blood or CSF, following a brain injury. UCH-L1 is a protein that is highly abundant in neurons and plays a critical role in protein degradation and synaptic function. It is involved in the processing of ubiquitin, a small regulatory protein that tags other proteins for degradation within the cell.

(In a cohort of trauma patients with normal mental status, GFAP outperformed UCH-L1 in detecting concussion in both children and adults. Blood levels of GFAP and UCH-L1 showed incremental elevations across three injury groups: from non-concussive body trauma, to non-concussive head trauma, to concussion.) BMJ Paediatr Open. 2019 Aug 25;3(1):e000473. doi: 10.1136/bmjpo-2019-000473. eCollection 2019.

MTHFR 677 G/G (Homozygous, "Wild Type" Reference Allele), 1298 G/G Homozygous, decreased activity allele), and TBI

Homocysteine levels are significantly inversely related with Montreal Cognitive Assessment (MoCA) scores. For mTBI, increases in homocysteine levels correlate with decreases in MoCA scores. mTBI patients with higher homocysteine are more likely to experience cognitive decline. Consider checking patient folate and homocysteine serum/plasma levels. Methyl Folate therapy may be useful to prevent hyperhomocysteinemia in homozygous mutant subjects. The MTHFR 1298 G/G genotype is associated with poor metabolic activity of the MTHFR enzyme.

Individuals that are homozygotes for the 1298 (G/G) variant are predisposed to hyperhomocysteinemia (high blood homocysteine levels) because they have less active MTHFR available to produce 5-methyltetrahydrofolate (which is used to decrease homocysteine). Due to this relationship with homocysteine, there is relevance to neurological, cardiovascular, and other diseases. Low dietary intake of the vitamin folate can also cause mild hyperhomocysteinemia. Low folate intake affects individuals with the 1298 A/A genotype to a greater extent than those with the 1298 (T/T) or (T/G) genotypes and lower plasma folate levels put the patient at risk for elevated plasma homocysteine levels

The MTHFR (methylenetetrahydrofolate reductase) gene provides instructions for making an enzyme that plays a crucial role in processing amino acids, the building blocks of proteins. Specifically, MTHFR is important for a chemical reaction involving the conversion of the amino acid homocysteine into methionine, which is necessary for DNA methylation and synthesis. Mutations in the MTHFR gene can lead to reduced activity of this enzyme, affecting homocysteine levels and folate metabolism, with potential implications for various health conditions, including cardiovascular diseases and complications during pregnancy. Folic acid can be bad as a replacement for folate, if this gene is activated.

FASEB J. 2018 Jan 5;32(4):1916–1932. doi: 10.1096/fj.201700826R

With MTHFR gene mutation. However, many individuals can't convert folic acid into methylfolate, leading to deficiency despite taking folic acid supplements.

In the context of traumatic brain injury (TBI), a positive finding for an MTHFR mutation—most commonly either the C677Tor A1298C mutation—has several implications:

1. Homocysteine Levels: MTHFR mutations can lead to elevated levels of homocysteine in the blood, a condition known as hyperhomocysteinemia. High homocysteine levels are associated with an increased risk of vascular diseases, including stroke, which can complicate recovery from TBI.

2. Neurological Recovery: There is some evidence to suggest that MTHFR mutations may impact neurological recovery following TBI. The altered folate metabolism could affect DNA repair mechanisms and neuronal recovery processes, potentially influencing the outcome after a brain injury. (Jacques et al, 1996).

APOE e3/e3 Patient Diplotype and TBI

APOE e3/e3 Genotype: Associated with better outcomes after injury and increased improvement in neuropsychological performance at 6 months postinjury than APOE e4 variant carriers

The e3 allele is correlated with better effects on cardiovascular disease and neurological health, neuroinflammation and in Alzheimer Disease than e4 carriers—e4 carriers have higher amyloid (Aβ) levels and amyloid plaque loads the in brain than non-e4 carriers. These e3/e3 patients tend to have better outcomes at 6 months postinjury than those that carry an e4 allele; it is expected that their improvement in neuropsychological performance at 6 months postinjury is also better than carriers of one or two copies of the e4 allele.

Most studied biomarkers and their current applications

Table 1 summarizes the main properties of the mostly studied biomarkers in the literature. Fig. 1, Fig. 2 show the expression of different blood biomarkers following TBI and their kinetic properties, respectively.

Table 1. Main properties of the mostly studied biomarkers in the literature.

Biomarker	Molecular weight (kDa)	Primary origin	Location	Other sources	Half–life (h)	Peak (h)
S100B	11	Astrocytes	Cytoplasm	Adipocytes, melanocytes, muscle, chondrocytes, enteric glial cells	0.5–2	<6
GFAP	50	Astrocytes	Cytoplasm	Schwann cells, chondrocytes, enteric glial cells liver, pancreas	24–48	20–24
UCH–L1	25	Neurons	Cytoplasm	Testis, ovary, kidney	8	7–9
Tau	33–46	Neurons	Axon terminals, unmyelinated axons	Astrocytes and oligodendrocytes, peripheral nervous system, kidneys	Unknown	12–24*
NF–L	68	Neurons	Myelinated axons	Peripheral axons	Unknown	Unknown

Glial fibrillary acidic protein (GFAP), Ubiquitin C-terminal hydrolase–L1 (UCH–L1), Neurofilament light (NF–L).

During trauma to the brain, a patient may experience a shearing, or tearing, of the long axonal connection fibers of the neuron used for communication between cells, a process called diffuse axonal injury (DAI). As NFs are released during neuroaxonal damage, and because they make up over 80% of all neuronal structural proteins, they can be used as sensitive indicators of DAI, the severity of which has important prognostic repercussions. Importantly, because diffusion tensor imaging (DTI) findings correlate with and help diagnose DAI, NF testing can lead imaging findings long before they may be seen on images and can serve as an early predictor of DTI findings and DAI severity.

The drug companies have yet to prove reducing Tau fixing anything, and in fact, studies have shown harm from the drug. The effectiveness of tau protein drugs for Alzheimer's disease is still under investigation. While some experimental drugs targeting tau proteins have shown promise in early studies, their overall effectiveness in clinical trials has been mixed. Tau Modification Drugs Take a Hit with Negative Trial | ALZFORUM: Nov 2024.

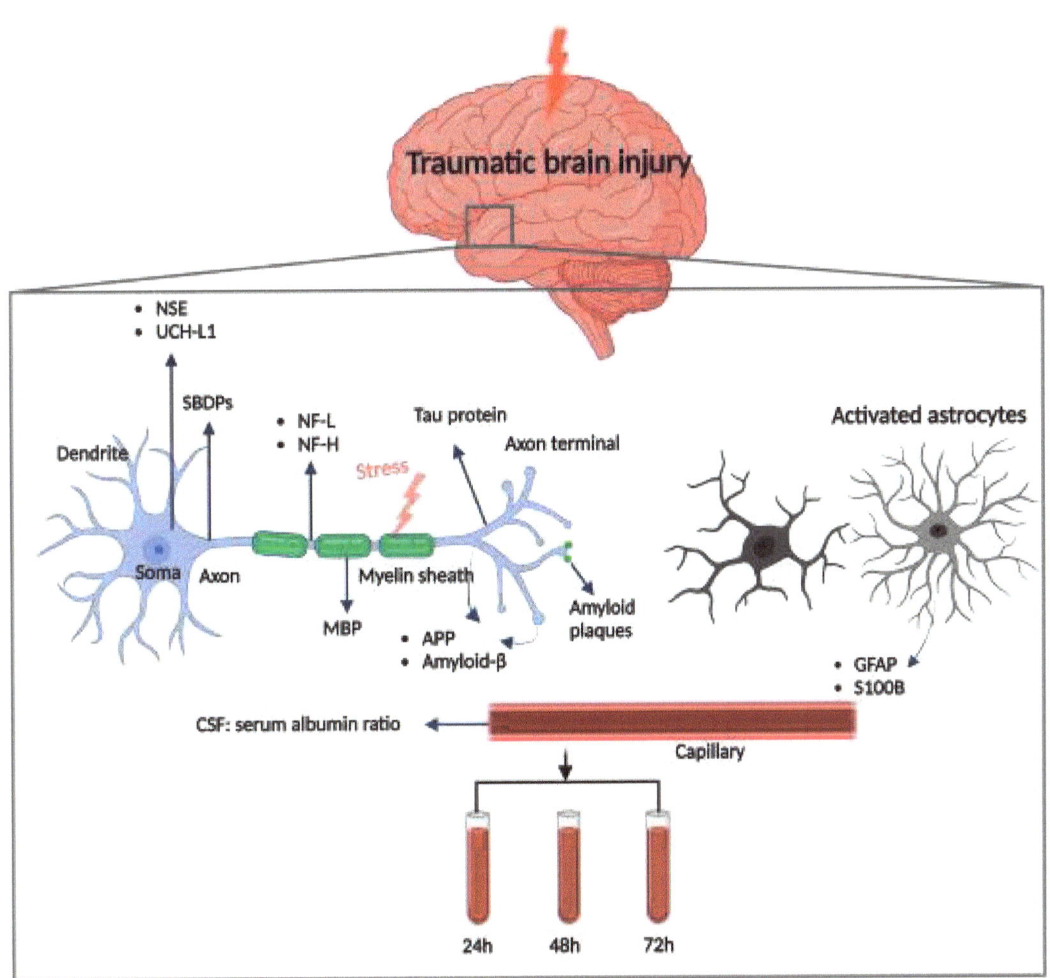

https://doi.org/10.1016/j.bas.2023.102735

How can I get this tested for my loved one?

The Neurotrauma Assessment Test (NAT) is an immunoassay that incorporates magnetic microspheres (beads) to enable the quantitative, multiplexed detection and measurement of GFAP (glial fibrillary acidic protein) and UCH–L1 (ubiquitin C–terminal hydrolase L1) in serum; it can be used in a single–plex form to detect GFAP or UCH–L1 independently, or in a multiplexed format to measure those proteins simultaneously. The assay uses antibody pairs (2 pairs) that recognize GFAP or UCH–L1 in an ELISA format using the magnetic colored bead technology from Luminex TM. Capture antibodies to GFAP or UCH–L1 are attached to two distinct bead sets with internal dyes colored differently for identifying GFAP and UCH–L1 independently; specific detection antibodies to GFAP and UCHL-1 are bound to fluorescent labels for quantifying the amount of the analytes in a sandwich interaction between the antibody pairs (capture and detection antibodies) and the analytes. A flow cell allows the beads and labels to be detected using lasers or light emitting diodes (LEDs) and high–speed detectors and digital signal processors for quantifying the sandwich–antibody, binding interactions on the GFAP and UCH–L1 analytes separately.

Additionally, Healix Pathology, Bellaire, TX 77401. (281) 846–6723 ·support@healixpathology.com, is currently offering this test to the patients of informed doctors, especially in Personal Injury cases.

MEDICAL DRUGS FOR TBI CURRENTLY

INF After a traumatic brain injury (TBI), inflammation can occur in the brain, which can lead to further damage. Certain medications, known as inflammation (INF) blockers, can help manage this inflammation and potentially improve outcomes123.

- **Infliximab**: Infliximab is a monoclonal anti–TNF–α antibody that reduces inflammation. Tumor necrotizing factor alpha (TNF–α) plays a crucial role in neuroinflammation post–TBI. TNF–α acts as the initiator of downstream inflammatory signaling pathways, and its activation can trigger a series of inflammatory reactions3. *****see below

- **Alpha– and Beta–Blockers**: A cocktail of alpha– and beta–blockers can suppress the adrenergic storm that occurs in the brain post–TBI. This re–opens the vessels that drain out of the brain and into the lymphatic system, removing excess fluid and debris from the site of injury and relieving pressure on the brain4.

- Other Pharmacotherapies: Other anti–inflammatory pharmacotherapies capable of attenuating the dysregulated inflammatory response along the brain–gut axis in TBI include hormones such as serotonin, ghrelin, and progesterone, ANS regulators such as beta–blockers, lipid–lowering drugs like statins, and intestinal flora modulators such as probiotics and antibiotics1.

https://doi.org/10.1016/B978–0–12–802686–1.00007–9 >>>

New Therapeutics for Traumatic Brain Injury

Prevention of Secondary Brain Damage and Enhancement of Repair and Regeneration 2017, Pages 109–129

Accumulating evidence suggests that chronic post–stroke **intracerebral microglial** activation and neuroinflammation, mediated by pathologic levels of tumor necrosis factor, constitute new therapeutic targets that **may persist for years after a stroke.**

Experimental data suggest that Etanercept, a selective TNF inhibitor, may ameliorate microglial activation; modulate the adverse synaptic effects of excess TNF; and favorably intervene in basic science models of TBI, stroke, subarachnoid hemorrhage, and Alzheimer's disease. Perispinal administration is a therapeutic method designed to use the cerebrospinal venous system to enhance selective delivery of etanercept across the blood–cerebrospinal fluid barrier. Increasing clinical data suggests that perispinal Etanercept (PSE) has therapeutic utility for treatment of selected brain disorders associated with elevated TNF, including chronic neurological dysfunction following stroke and various forms of brain injury. PSE is an emerging treatment modality for TBI.

CNS Drugs. 2014; 28(8): 679–697.

Published online 2014 May 27. doi: 10.1007/s40263–014–0174–2

Perispinal Etanercept is a promising treatment for the chronic neurologic dysfunction that may persist after resolution of acute COVID–19, including chronic cognitive dysfunction, fatigue, and depression. These results suggest that long COVID brain neuroinflammation is a potentially reversible pathology and viable treatment target. https://doi.org/10.1080/03007995.2022.2096351

What else is newer in the Medical treatment of TBI?

- **Neural Exosomes for TBI**: Researchers at the University of Georgia have developed a new technology using neural exosomes to treat traumatic brain injury (TBI). These exosomes can minimize or avert TBI progression by resetting and regenerating communication between cells.

- **Non-Invasive Treatment**: The treatment involves injecting bio-manufactured exosomes intravenously, offering a non-invasive alternative to brain surgery.

- **Potential Applications**: This technology could be used for immediate treatment of severe TBI and as a preventive measure for mild and moderate concussions.

- **Commercial Development**: The technology is being developed by Aruna Bio and has received significant financial support, including $13 million in common stock financing.

- *Journal of Neuroinflammation* **volume 21**, Article number: 124 (2024)

****

(Recent research has shown that **aqueous cinnamon extract (aCE)**, particularly from **Cinnamomum cassia**, acts synergistically with **infliximab**, an anti-TNF-α biotherapeutic, to mitigate inflammation. This combination has shown promise as a complementary and alternative medicine (CAM) to improve patients' quality of life, especially for those who are non-responders to infliximab

An in vitro study elucidating the synergistic effects of aqueous cinnamon extract and an anti-TNF-α biotherapeutic: implications for a complementary and alternative therapy for non-responders. *BMC Complement Med Ther* **24**, 131 (2024). https://doi.org/10.1186/s12906-024-04438-w

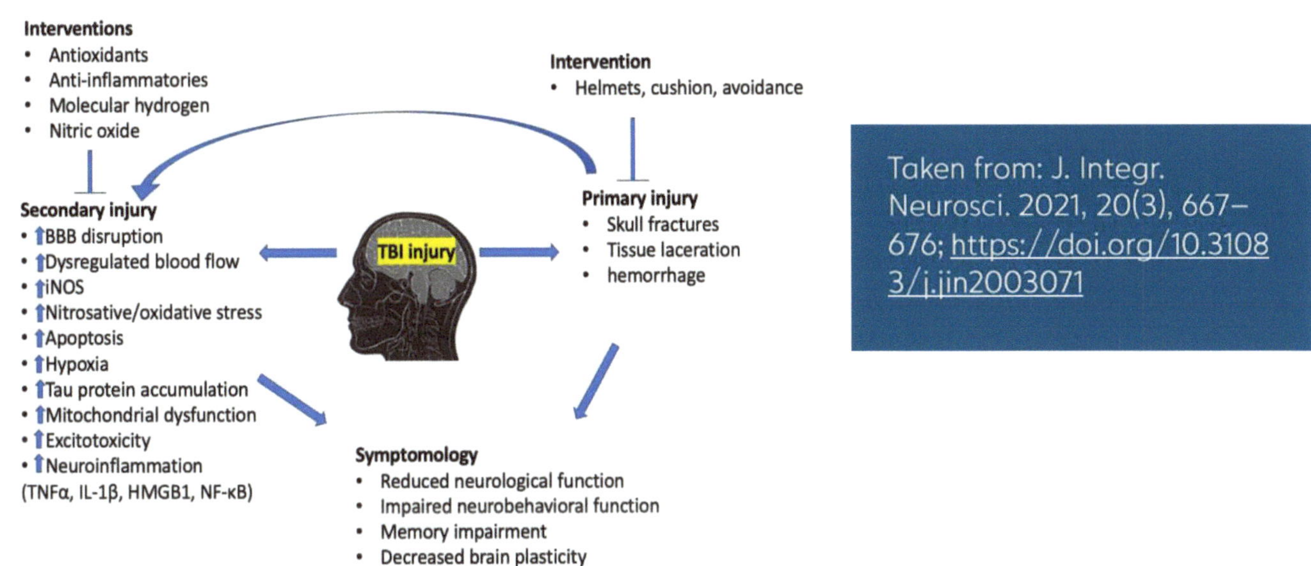

They discharged me, but what should I do the next 24 hours to minimize future problems?

Most ERs (now called EDs) and hospitals don't recommend something immediately after discharge to help? So many systems are affected, that they don't have time to check. Pathetic!

SO you can deal with with alternative and complimentary medicine. Lets find out how.

The reason I wrote this book was to fill in the gaps of current brain care. So let's dive in:

TBI leads to bacterial and hormonal imbalance in the gastrointestinal (GI) tract.

Studies have suggested that TBI can lead to bacterial imbalance (dysbiosis) and hormonal disturbances in the GI tract. Here are five examples supported by findings from professional journals:

TBI has been associated with changes in the composition of gut microbiota, leading to dysbiosis. Research has shown that TBI-induced stress responses, including alterations in autonomic nervous system activity and changes in intestinal permeability, can disrupt the balance of beneficial and pathogenic bacteria in the gut.

Reference: Houlden, A., Goldrick, M., Brough, D., Vizi, E. S., Lénárt, N., Martinecz, B., ... & Denes, A. (2016). Brain injury induces specific changes in the caecal microbiota of mice via altered autonomic activity and mucoprotein production. Brain, Behavior, and Immunity, 57, 10–20. doi:10.1016/j.bbi.2016.04.005

Increased Intestinal Permeability: TBI can disrupt the integrity of the intestinal barrier, leading to increased permeability and leakage of bacterial toxins into systemic circulation. This phenomenon, known as "leaky gut," has been implicated in the pathogenesis of systemic inflammation and immune dysregulation following TBI.

Reference: Sharma, R., Yang, T., Oliveira, A. C., Aquino, V., Zhang, X., & Tobe, B. (2020). A Review of the Systemic and Neurological Effects of Gut Microbiota Alterations in Human and Rodent Models of Traumatic Brain Injury. Frontiers in Neurology, 11, 627. doi:10.3389/fneur.2020.00627

Disrupted Gut-Brain Axis Communication: TBI-induced alterations in gut microbiota and intestinal permeability can disrupt bidirectional communication along the gut-brain axis. Dysregulated signaling between the gut and the central nervous system may contribute to neuroinflammation, cognitive impairment, and mood disturbances observed in individuals with TBI.

Reference: Flierl, M. A., Stahel, P. F., Beauchamp, K. M., Morgan, S. J., Smith, W. R., Shohami, E., & Tarkowski, E. (2009). Mouse closed head injury model induced by a weight-drop device. Nature Protocols, 4(9), 1328–1337. doi:10.1038/nprot.2009.148

Hormonal Dysregulation: TBI can disrupt the hypothalamic-pituitary-adrenal (HPA) axis, leading to dysregulation of hormonal signaling in the GI tract. Alterations in cortisol and other stress-related hormones may impact gut motility, mucosal integrity, and immune function, contributing to GI symptoms commonly observed in individuals with TBI.

Reference: D'Mello, C., Ronaghan, N., Zaheer, R., Dicay, M., Le, T., MacNaughton, W. K., ... & Swain, M. G. (2015). Probiotics Improve Inflammation-Associated Sickness Behavior by Altering Communication between the Peripheral Immune System and the Brain. Journal of Neuroscience, 35(30), 10821–10830. doi:10.1523/JNEUROSCI.0575-15.2015

Immune Dysregulation and Inflammation: TBI-induced alterations in the gut microbiota and intestinal barrier function can trigger systemic immune responses and low-grade inflammation. Chronic activation of the immune system in the gut may contribute to the development of GI disorders, such as irritable bowel syndrome (IBS), in individuals with a history of TBI.

Reference: Flierl, M. A., Stahel, P. F., Beauchamp, K. M., Morgan, S. J., Smith, W. R., Shohami, E., ... & Tarkowski, E. (2009). Mouse closed head injury model induced by a weight-drop device. Nature Protocols, 4(9), 1328–1337. doi:10.1038/nprot.2009.148.

The specific changes in gut bacteria (microbiota) following traumatic brain injury (TBI) can vary depending on factors such as the severity of the injury, individual differences, and the duration of follow-up. However, several studies have identified alterations in the composition and diversity of gut microbiota associated with TBI. Some changes include:

Decreased Diversity: TBI has been associated with a decrease in the overall diversity of gut microbiota, characterized by a reduction in the abundance and richness of microbial species. This decrease in diversity may contribute to dysbiosis and impaired gut function.

Shifts in Microbial Composition: TBI can lead to shifts in the relative abundance of specific bacterial taxa in the gut. While the exact patterns may vary, some studies have reported an increase in potentially pathogenic bacteria such as Enterobacteriaceae and a decrease in beneficial bacteria such as Lactobacillus and Bifidobacterium.

Increased Inflammation–Associated Bacteria: TBI–induced alterations in gut microbiota may promote the expansion of bacteria associated with inflammation and immune dysregulation. For example, an increase in Proteobacteria, which includes several pro–inflammatory taxa, has been observed in individuals with TBI.

Reduced SCFA–Producing Bacteria: Short–chain fatty acids (SCFAs) produced by certain gut bacteria play a crucial role in gut health and immune regulation. TBI has been linked to a decrease in SCFA–producing bacteria such as Faecalibacterium prausnitzii and Butyricicoccus, which may contribute to gut dysbiosis and inflammation.

Altered Gut–Brain Axis Signaling: TBI–induced changes in gut microbiota can disrupt communication along the gut–brain axis, influencing neuroinflammation, neurotransmitter synthesis, and behavior. Dysregulated gut–brain signaling may exacerbate TBI–related symptoms such as cognitive impairment and mood disturbances.

It's important to note that the mechanisms underlying these changes in gut microbiota following TBI are complex and multifactorial. Factors such as alterations in gut motility, intestinal permeability, and immune function may contribute to dysbiosis and microbial imbalance.

References to scientific literature that discuss the alterations in gut microbiota following traumatic brain injury (TBI) and the associated changes in microbial composition. Here are references for the points mentioned:

Decreased Diversity: Cryan, J. F., & Dinan, T. G. (2012). Mind–altering microorganisms: the impact of the gut microbiota on brain and behaviour. Nature Reviews Neuroscience, 13(10), 701–712. doi:10.1038/nrn3346

Shifts in Microbial Composition: Benakis, C., Martin-Gallausiaux, C., Trezzi, J. P., Melton, P., Liesz, A., Wilmes, P., & Thevenet, J. (2020). The microbiome–gut–brain axis in acute and chronic brain diseases. Current Opinion in Neurobiology, 61, 1–9. doi:10.1016/j.conb.2019.11.006

Increased Inflammation–Associated Bacteria: Stanley, D., Mason, L. J., Mackin, K. E., Srikhanta, Y. N., Lyras, D., Prakash, M. D., ... & Moore, R. J. (2016). Translocation and dissemination of commensal bacteria in post–stroke infection. Nature Medicine, 22(11), 1277–1284. doi:10.1038/nm.4194

Reduced SCFA–Producing Bacteria: Sun, M. F., Zhu, Y. L., Zhou, Z. L., Jia, X. B., Xu, Y. D., Yang, Q., ... & Chen, L. L. (2018). Neuroprotective effects of fecal microbiota transplantation on MPTP–induced Parkinson's disease mice: Gut microbiota, glial reaction and TLR4/TNF-α signaling pathway. Brain, Behavior, and Immunity, 70, 48–60. doi:10.1016/j.bbi.2017.12.017

Altered Gut-Brain Axis Signaling: Grenham, S., Clarke, G., Cryan, J. F., & Dinan, T. G. (2011). Brain-gut-microbe communication in health and disease. Frontiers in Physiology, 2, 94. doi:10.3389/fphys.2011.00094

Nutritional care for Brain injury from stoke, concussion, or aging. The caveat is they have to get thru the damaged BBB (blood Brain Barrier).

Herbs That Cross the Blood–Brain Barrier

Ginkgo Biloba: Known for its neuroprotective properties, ginkgo biloba improves blood flow to the brain and enhances cognitive function. It contains flavonoids and terpenoids that can cross the BBB and aid in TBI recovery.

Reference: Kennedy, D. O. (2000). Herbal extracts and phytochemicals: Plant secondary metabolites and the enhancement of human brain function. Advances in Nutrition Research, 10(Supplement C), 47–73. https://doi.org/10.1016/s1054-3589(00)80008-6

Bacopa Monnieri: This adaptogenic herb has been used in traditional medicine to improve memory, reduce anxiety, and support overall brain health. It contains bacosides, which have been found to enhance neuronal communication and protect against oxidative stress.

Reference: Stough, C., Downey, L. A., Lloyd, J., Silber, B., Redman, S., Hutchison, C., & Wesnes, K. (2008). Examining the cognitive effects of a special extract of Bacopa monniera (CDRI 08: KeenMind): A review of ten years of research at Swinburne University. Journal of Pharmacy & Pharmaceutical Sciences, 11(3), 325–354.

Combining Herbs and Amino Acids for Synergistic Effects. Supplements related to Traumatic Brain Injury (TBI) treatment.

While herbs and amino acids offer individual benefits, combining them can often result in synergistic effects, enhancing their overall efficacy in TBI recovery. For example, combining ginkgo biloba with acetyl-L-carnitine may provide comprehensive support for brain health and cognitive function.

Amino Acids That Cross the Blood–Brain Barrier

L-Theanine: Found in green tea, L-theanine promotes relaxation without causing drowsiness. It crosses the blood–brain barrier and increases levels of neurotransmitters such as dopamine and serotonin, which play essential roles in mood regulation and cognitive function.

Reference: Nobre, A. C., Rao, A., & Owen, G. N. (2008). L-theanine, a natural constituent in tea, and its effect on mental state. Asia Pacific Journal of Clinical Nutrition, 17(S1), 167–168.

Acetyl-L-Carnitine: This amino acid derivative enhances mitochondrial function and energy production in the brain. It has shown promise in improving cognitive function and reducing neuronal damage following brain injury.

Reference: Montgomery, S. A., & Thal, L. J. (1991). Acetyl-L-carnitine in the treatment of Alzheimer's disease. Acta Neurologica Scandinavica, 84(1), 8–11. https://doi.org/10.1111/j.1600-0404.1991.tb04976.x

Additionally, the use of Nitric Oxide, Ginger, Apigenin, Rutin, and Resveratrol to bypass the Blood–Brain Barrier (BBB) in Traumatic Brain Injury (TBI)

Nitric Oxide (NO): Vasodilation: Nitric oxide acts as a potent vasodilator, increasing blood flow to the brain and potentially enhancing the delivery of therapeutic agents across the blood–brain barrier.

Neuroprotection: NO exhibits neuroprotective properties by modulating oxidative stress, inflammation, and excitotoxicity, thereby mitigating secondary brain injury following TBI.

Reference: Wei, E. P., Kontos, H. A., & Beckman, J. S. (1996). Mechanisms of cerebral vasodilation by superoxide, hydrogen peroxide, and peroxynitrite. American Journal of Physiology–Heart and Circulatory Physiology, 271(3), H1262–H1266. doi:10.1152/ajpheart.1996.271.3.H1262

Ginger (Zingiber officinale):

Anti–inflammatory Effects: Ginger contains bioactive compounds with anti–inflammatory properties that may help reduce BBB permeability and inflammation in the brain following TBI.

Neuroprotection: Ginger extract has shown neuroprotective effects in animal studies, potentially mitigating neuronal damage and improving functional outcomes after TBI.

Reference: Saenghong, N., Wattanathorn, J., Muchimapura, S., Tongun, T., Piyavhatkul, N., Banchonglikitkul, C., & Kajsongkram, T. (2012). Zingiber officinale Improves Cognitive Function of the Middle–Aged Healthy Women. Evidence–Based Complementary and Alternative Medicine, 2012, 1–7. doi:10.1155/2012/383062

Apigenin: BBB Permeability Enhancement: Apigenin, a flavonoid found in various plants, has been shown to enhance BBB permeability, potentially facilitating the delivery of therapeutic agents to the brain.

Anti–inflammatory and Antioxidant Effects: Apigenin possesses anti–inflammatory and antioxidant properties that may help mitigate neuroinflammation and oxidative stress associated with TBI.

Reference: Wang, X., Li, T., Li, J., Zhang, T., Yu, W., & Zhang, Y. (2016). Apigenin Protects Against Acute Cerebral Ischemia/Reperfusion Injury by Inhibiting Neuronal Apoptosis. Experimental and Therapeutic Medicine, 12(6), 3639–3645. doi:10.3892/etm.2016.3835

Rutin: Antioxidant Activity: Rutin, a flavonoid glycoside, exhibits potent antioxidant activity, which may help protect brain cells from oxidative damage and preserve BBB integrity following TBI.

Anti–inflammatory Effects: Rutin has anti–inflammatory properties that may attenuate neuroinflammation and secondary brain injury cascades associated with TBI.

Reference: Siddiqui, S., Ahsan, H., & Khan, M. R. (2011). Rutin Prevents Cognitive Impairments by Ameliorating Oxidative Stress and Neuroinflammation in Rat Model of Lead–Induced Alzheimer's Disease. NeuroToxicology, 32(3), 215–226. doi:10.1016/j.neuro.2010.12.009

Resveratrol: BBB Permeability Enhancement: Resveratrol, a polyphenol found in red wine and grapes, has been shown to modulate BBB permeability, potentially allowing for the delivery of therapeutic agents to the brain.

Neuroprotection: Resveratrol exhibits neuroprotective effects through its antioxidant, anti–inflammatory, and anti-apoptotic properties, which may mitigate neuronal damage and improve outcomes following TBI.

Reference: Kulkarni, S. K., & Dhir, A. (2008). An Overview of Curcumin in Neurological Disorders. Indian Journal of Pharmaceutical Sciences, 70(5), 620–623. doi:10.4103/0250-474X.44591

Oregano: Carvacrol (2-methyl-5-(1-methyl ethyl)-phenol) (CAR) is found in oils obtained from the plants of the Lamiaceae family, such as *Tym*, *Satureja*, and *Origanum* genera, in concentrations of 85–90% [1,2] . Because of its low molecular mass and lipophilic characteristics, this molecule may easily pass across the blood–brain barrier (BBB) [3] .

CAR is generally considered a safe food additive that can be added directly to human food [4,5] and possesses various beneficial effects in vitro and in vivo, including antioxidant, anticancer, antibacterial, antifungal, anti-inflammatory, and hepatoprotective properties [6–9] . Recent studies have shown that CAR exerts its neuroprotective effects in brain disorders by inhibiting reactive oxygen species (ROS) production and antioxidant properties.

Methylene Blue: MB is a thiophenazine dye with FDA approval for treating several illnesses. Its ease in crossing the blood–brain barrier and potential therapeutic use in central nervous system diseases have increased interest in its application for treating ALZHEIMER'S DISEASE. The literature reviews include randomized clinical trials investigating MB's potential benefits in treating AD. The findings of the studies indicate that the administration of MB has demonstrated enhancements in cognitive function, reductions in the accumulation of plaques containing beta-amyloid, improvements in memory and cognitive function in animal subjects, and possesses antioxidant properties that can mitigate oxidative stress and inflammation within the brain. Brain Pathol . 2011 Jan 27;21(2):140–149. doi: 10.1111/j.1750-3639.2010.00430.x

TNF and inflammation reducers:

Research data from January 2022, can outline some of the potential benefits of turmeric, Chinese skullcap, glutathione, and ATP supplements for TBI.

Turmeric (Curcumin):

Anti-inflammatory Properties: Curcumin, the active compound in turmeric, has potent anti-inflammatory effects. Studies suggest that it may help reduce inflammation in the brain following a TBI, potentially minimizing secondary damage.

Antioxidant Activity: Turmeric exhibits strong antioxidant activity, which can help protect brain cells from oxidative stress and damage caused by free radicals.

Neuroprotective Effects: Research indicates that curcumin may have neuroprotective properties, supporting the survival of neurons and promoting brain repair mechanisms.

Improved Cognitive Function: Some studies suggest that turmeric supplementation may enhance cognitive function, memory, and overall brain health, which could be beneficial for individuals recovering from a TBI. *J Neuroinflammation* **11**, 59 (2014). https://doi.org/10.1186/1742-2094-11-59

Chinese Skullcap (Scutellaria baicalensis):

Anti-inflammatory Effects: Chinese skullcap contains bioactive compounds with potent anti-inflammatory properties, which may help reduce inflammation in the brain following a TBI and alleviate associated symptoms.

Neuroprotective Potential: Preliminary research suggests that Chinese skullcap may exert neuroprotective effects by modulating various cellular pathways involved in brain injury and repair.

Antioxidant Activity: Like turmeric, Chinese skullcap exhibits antioxidant activity, which can help protect brain cells from oxidative damage and support overall brain health during the recovery process.

Cognitive Support: While more research is needed, some studies have suggested that Chinese skullcap may support cognitive function and memory, potentially benefiting individuals recovering from a TBI.

Wei, C., Wang, J., Yu, J. *et al.* Therapy of traumatic brain injury by modern agents and traditional Chinese medicine. *Chin Med* **18**, 25 (2023). https://doi.org/10.1186/s13020-023-00731-x

Glutathione: (ONE OF MY FAVORITES!)

Antioxidant Defense: Glutathione is a powerful endogenous antioxidant that plays a crucial role in protecting cells, including brain cells, from oxidative stress. Supplementing with glutathione may enhance the brain's antioxidant defense mechanisms, potentially reducing oxidative damage associated with TBIs.

Anti-inflammatory Effects: Glutathione has been shown to possess anti-inflammatory properties, which may help mitigate inflammation in the brain following injury and contribute to the healing process.

Neuroprotection: Research suggests that glutathione may have neuroprotective effects, supporting neuronal survival and function, and potentially aiding in the repair of damaged brain tissue after a TBI.

Enhanced Recovery: Some studies have indicated that glutathione supplementation may promote faster recovery and improved outcomes in individuals with TBIs, although more research is needed to confirm these effects conclusively. Glutathione * SEAL Future Foundation

ATP (Adenosine Triphosphate) Supplements:

Energy Support: ATP is the primary energy currency of cells, including neurons in the brain. Supplementing with ATP or its precursors may help support energy production in brain cells, potentially enhancing cellular function and promoting recovery after a TBI.

Neurotransmitter Regulation: ATP plays a role in the regulation of neurotransmitter release and synaptic transmission. By supporting optimal neurotransmitter function, ATP supplements may contribute to improved cognitive function and overall brain health during TBI recovery.

Neuroprotective Effects: Some research suggests that ATP supplementation may have neuroprotective effects, helping to preserve neuronal integrity and function in the face of injury or damage.

Cognitive Enhancement: While more studies are needed, preliminary research has shown promising results regarding the potential cognitive-enhancing effects of ATP supplementation, which could be beneficial for individuals recovering from TBIs. Nitric oxide products are available in liposomal form for best absorption, and convert to ATP.

TUDCA: TUDCA inhibits multiple proteins involved in apoptosis and upregulates cell survival pathways. In addition, TUDCA exhibits anti-inflammatory effects in models of neuroinflammation and attenuates neuronal loss in chronic neurodegenerative diseases. This may be applicable to TBI, which also triggers inflammatory and apoptotic processes. Additionally, preliminary data support the use of pharmacological therapies that reduce apoptosis and inflammation associated with TBI.*

Application of Tauroursodeoxycholic Acid for Treatment of Neurological and Non-neurological Diseases: Is There a Potential for Treating Traumatic Brain Injury?

Kyle R. Gronbeck, Cecilia M P Rodrigues, Javad Mahmoudi, Eric M. Bershad, Geoffrey Ling, Salam P. Bachour, Afshin A. Divani

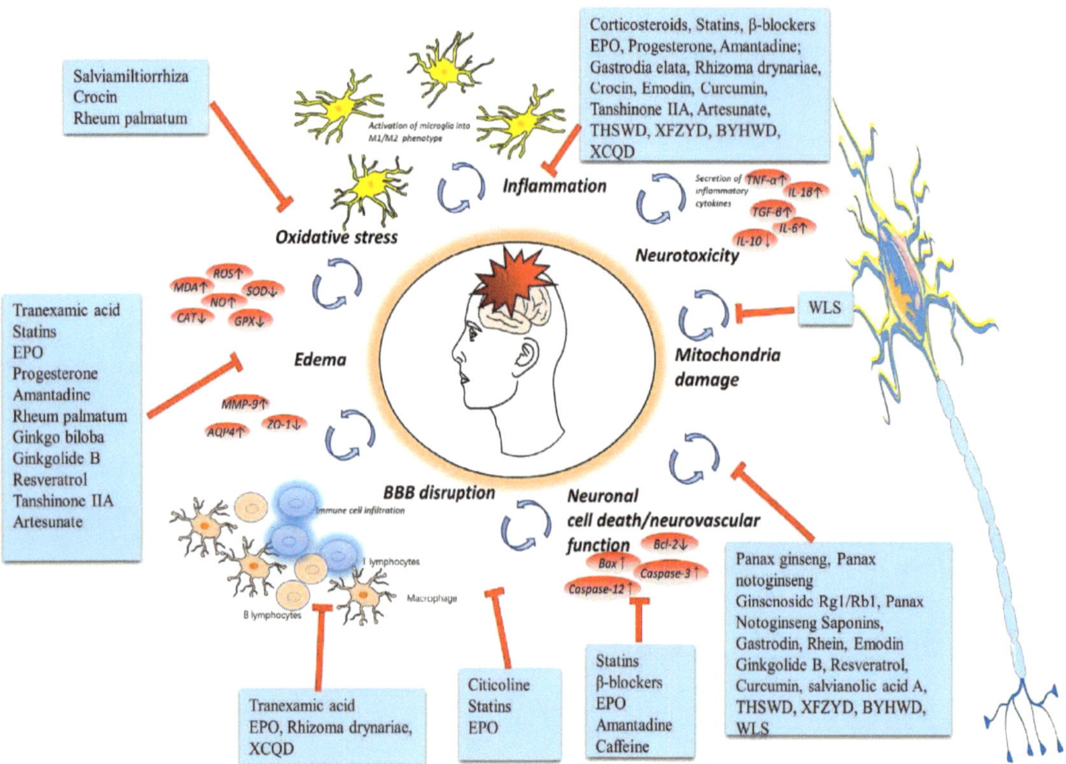

Wei, C., Wang, J., Yu, J. *et al.* Therapy of traumatic brain injury by modern agents and traditional Chinese medicine. *Chin Med* **18**, 25 (2023). https://doi.org/10.1186/s13020-023-00731-x

DOSAGES:

Nutrition:

An IV therapy package can include crucial vitamins and minerals to strengthen the body's systems and improve overall health. IV therapy treatments often deliver some combination of immune-boosting nutrients like vitamin C, vitamin B12, calcium, magnesium or glutathione, which is a powerful antioxidant.

When it comes to **IV nutrient therapy**, various formulations exist. An example is the popular **Myers' cocktail**, which includes:

- Magnesium: 2 to 5 mL

- Calcium: 1 to 3 mL

- Vitamin B6: 1 mL

- Vitamin B12: 1 mL

- Vitamin B5: 1 mL

- Vitamin B complex: 1 mL[1]

Glutathione, a powerful antioxidant, can be beneficial for **traumatic brain injury (TBI)** recovery. Here are some dosage guidelines:

1. **IV Injections**: Typically, IV glutathione doses range from **600 to 1200 milligrams** per session, administered once or twice a week[1].

2. **Liposomal Glutathione**: For liposomal forms, a general guideline is **500–2000 mg** per day, starting with a low dose and gradually increasing[2].

3. **Peptide Administration**: Clinicians recommend about **600 mg weekly**, split into six injections throughout the week[3].

4. **Daily Dosage**: Studies show positive results with **250–300 mg** daily, but therapeutic doses may vary[4].

Inhaled nitric oxide (iNO) can be beneficial for **traumatic brain injury (TBI)** patients. Here are the key points regarding its use:

1. **Recommended Dose**: The typical dose is **20 parts per million (ppm)**, maintained for up to **14 days** or until oxygen desaturation resolves.

2. **Weaning Off**: To discontinue, down-titrate gradually in several steps, pausing at each step to monitor for hypoxemia[1].

3. **Caution**: Doses above 20 ppm are **not recommended**[1].

4. APEX energetics sells this in liposomal form through Functional Medicine Chiropractors.

The recommended dosage of **turmeric** for **traumatic brain injury (TBI)** varies based on the specific conditions. Here are some guidelines:

- To combat inflammation, consider **500 to 1,000 milligrams** of curcuminoids daily, or up to **2,000 milligrams**. https://www.wellandgood.com/turmeric-anti-inflammatory-dosage

- Start with a lower dose and gradually increase as needed.

When considering **Lactobacillus** and **Bifidobacterium** probiotics after a **traumatic brain injury (TBI)**, here are some general guidelines:

1. **Lactobacillus:**

   - **Usual Adult Dose**: **1 capsule** orally daily.

   - Consider products containing at least **5 billion colony-forming units (CFUs)** per day for effectiveness.

2. **Bifidobacterium:**

   - **Usual Adult Dose**: **1 tablet** chewed daily1.

Look for products with adequate CFUs to achieve clinical benefits 2

PROBIOTICS FOR GASTROINTESTINAL CONDITIONS:

A Summary of the Evidence *Am Fam Physician.* 2017;96(3):170–178

Omega-3 fatty acids from fish oil can be beneficial for **traumatic brain injury (TBI)** recovery. Here are some dosage guidelines:

1. **Initial High Dose (First 7 Days)**:

   - Take **3000 mg** of EPA + DHA three times a day.

   - This level exceeds most government health body recommendations, so consult your doctor1.

2. **Maintenance Dose (Week 2 and beyond)**:

   - Reduce to **3000 mg** of EPA + DHA twice a day1.

     Dr. Michael Lewis, directs the non-profit **Brain Health Education and Research Institute** in Potomac, Maryland. He, along with Drs Barry Sears, Joe Hibbeln and Julian Bales are the handful of leading authorities in this field.

*Diverse neurodegenerative conditions share some common features, such as neuronal loss, disordered protein aggregation, mitochondrial dysfunction, and oxidative stress. TUDCA, which is one of the most hydrophilic of the bile acids, is able to cross the blood-brain barrier, and potentially exert neuroprotective effects in ways that mitigate many of these neurodegenerative mechanisms.

1. **TUDCA (Tauroursodeoxycholic Acid)**: Around 500 mg per day.
2. **Chinese Skullcap (Scutellaria baicalensis)**: Typical dosage is 1–3 grams of the dried root per day.
3. **Methylene Blue**: Low doses are around 0.5–4 mg per kg of body weight. The half-life of oral methylene blue is 4 to 6 hours
4. **Carvacrol (from Oregano Oil)**: 200 mg per day.
5. **Resveratrol**: 250–500 mg per day.
6. **Rutin**: 500 mg per day.
7. **Ginger**: 1–2 grams per day.
8. **Apigenin**: 50 mg per day.
9. **L-Theanine**: 100–200 mg per day.
10. **Acetyl L-Carnitine**: 500–1,500 mg per day.
11. **Phosphatidylserine**: 100–300 mg per day.
12. **Ginkgo Biloba**

- **Dosage**: 240–480 mg per day of standardized extract (24% flavonoid glycosides).
- **Usage**: Often divided into smaller doses throughout the day.

13. **Turmeric (Curcumin)**
- **Dosage**: 500–2,000 mg per day of curcumin extract.
- **Usage**: Best taken with meals to enhance absorption.

14. **Bacopa Monnieri**
- **Dosage**: 300–450 mg per day of standardized extract (55% bacosides).
- **Usage**: Consistent daily use is recommended for best results

USING A KETOGENIC DIET FOR TRAUMATIC BRAIN INJURY

A ketogenic diet may also be recommended for some survivors of brain injury. Although this diet tends to be more restrictive than most, many of the foods promoted in the ketogenic diet are low in carbs and processed sugars and high in fat and protein, which are essential for brain injury recovery. While the effects of a ketogenic diet on brain injury recovery are still being researched, animal studies have shown that consuming a ketogenic diet after TBI can result in reduced cerebral edema and apoptosis (cell death), as well as improved cerebral metabolism and behavioral outcomes.

One of the stranger effects of TBI is the way it impairs the brain's ability to convert glucose into energy. Glucose is the primary fuel source of the brain and without it, the brain cannot function efficiently. Therefore, after a brain injury, it is vital that you find some other source of energy to help your brain heal. This alternate source can come in the form of **ketones**.

Ketones are a type of acid that your liver produces from fat. The benefit of ketones is that, unlike glucose, your brain can easily convert them into energy after a TBI. The best way to produce ketones is to get your body into a state of **ketosis**. This is a normal metabolic process that is triggered when your body doesn't have enough carbs to burn for energy. Instead, your body burns fat, and this creates ketones.

To trigger ketosis, you must consume a low-carb diet, also known as a ketogenic diet. Ketogenic diets have been shown to improve cognition and boost recovery in animals with traumatic brain injury. Studies are still forthcoming but there seems to be a lot of promise.

When on a ketogenic diet, the foods you eat must have a low-carb count but be high in fat and protein. The following are some good examples of food that meet these requirements:

- Plain Greek yogurt

- Cottage cheese

- Eggs

- Avocado

- Olive oil

If these foods do not appeal to you, that is fine. A ketogenic diet is not a necessary part of brain injury recovery. As long as you are receiving the nutrients listed in the section above, your nutrition therapy will be a success.

How Ketogenic Diets Curb Inflammation in the Brain | UC San Francisco (ucsf.edu)

Role of Music Therapy in Traumatic Brain Injury: A Systematic Review and Meta-analysis

Music therapy is not a new concept.

Music has the unique ability to stimulate sensory, motor, perceptive-cognitive and emotional functions simultaneously within the brain. This results in the activation of numerous areas of the brain, in both the right and the left hemispheres.

Consistently stimulating the brain activates a process referred to as neuroplasticity. Through neuroplasticity, the brain can reorganize neural pathways in response to changes in the environment or experience. Therefore, when experiencing music, whether as an active participant or passive listener, adaptive rewiring in the brain may be taking place. The brain then compensates for lost functions by reassigning these functions to undamaged brain regions. Consistent, repetitive tasks and experiences are the best way to activate neuroplasticity.

"Music therapy has promising results in improving rehabilitation outcomes of patients with various neurologic disorders; Pooled results from 6 studies demonstrated statistically significant improvement in the stride length and executive function outcome in patients with TBI after music therapy rehabilitation."

World Neurosurg. 2021 Feb:146:197-204. doi: 10.1016/j.wneu.2020.10.130. Epub 2020 Oct 29.

THE ROLE OF CHIROPRACTIC CARE IN TBI DIAGNOSIS AND TREATMENT

Traumatic brain injuries (TBIs) present complex challenges in diagnosis and treatment. While medical doctors (MDs) play a crucial role in TBI management, chiropractors offer unique perspectives and techniques that can complement traditional medical approaches. In this chapter, we explore how chiropractic care can be useful for diagnosing and treating TBIs in ways that MDs may not.

Diagnostic Advantages of Chiropractic Care

Functional Assessment: Chiropractors are trained to assess the functional status of the nervous system, including the spine and cranial nerves. Through manual examinations and neurological assessments, chiropractors can identify subtle abnormalities that may indicate underlying brain injury, even in cases where imaging studies appear normal.

Comprehensive Evaluation: Chiropractors take a holistic approach to patient care, considering not only physical symptoms but also lifestyle factors, biomechanics, and environmental influences. This comprehensive evaluation allows chiropractors to identify contributing factors to TBI symptoms and develop individualized treatment plans.

Dynamic Imaging Techniques: While MDs typically rely on static imaging studies such as CT scans and MRIs, chiropractors may utilize dynamic imaging techniques such as digital motion X-ray (DMX) or videofluoroscopy to assess structural integrity and functional movement of the spine and surrounding tissues. These dynamic assessments can provide valuable insights into the mechanisms of injury and associated neurological dysfunction.

Treatment Modalities in Chiropractic Care for TBI

Spinal Manipulation: Chiropractic adjustments aim to restore proper alignment and function to the spine, which can have far-reaching effects on neurological function and overall health. By addressing subluxations (misalignments) in the spine, chiropractors may help alleviate symptoms associated with TBI, such as headaches, neck pain, and cognitive dysfunction.

Cranial Adjustments: Chiropractors trained in cranial adjusting techniques can gently manipulate the bones of the skull to improve cranial bone mobility and optimize cerebrospinal fluid flow. These adjustments may help relieve intracranial pressure, reduce inflammation, and promote healing in individuals with TBIs.

Neurological Rehabilitation: Chiropractors may incorporate specialized rehabilitation exercises and therapeutic modalities to support neurological recovery following a TBI. These modalities may include vestibular rehabilitation, balance training, eye movement exercises, and cognitive rehabilitation techniques tailored to the individual's specific needs.

Nutrition Advice: It's important to note that the mechanisms underlying changes in gut microbiota following TBI are complex and multifactorial. Factors such as alterations in gut motility, intestinal permeability, and immune function may contribute to dysbiosis and microbial imbalance.

Collaborative Care Approach: Chiropractors recognize the importance of interdisciplinary collaboration in TBI management. By working closely with medical doctors, neurologists, physical therapists, and other healthcare providers, chiropractors can ensure comprehensive care that addresses all aspects of the patient's condition. Chiropractic care offers valuable contributions to the diagnosis and treatment of TBIs, complementing traditional medical approaches with specialized assessments and interventions. Through functional assessment techniques, dynamic imaging modalities, and targeted treatment strategies, chiropractors play a vital role in supporting neurological recovery and optimizing outcomes for individuals with TBIs.

References: Hawk, C., Schneider, M., Ferrance, R. J., Hewitt, E., & Van Loon, M. (2009). Best practices recommendations for chiropractic care for infants, children, and adolescents: results of a consensus process. Journal of Manipulative and Physiological Therapeutics, 32(8), 639–647. doi:10.1016/j.jmpt.2009.08.018

Haavik, H., & Murphy, B. (2012). The role of spinal manipulation in addressing disordered sensorimotor integration and altered motor control. Journal of Electromyography and Kinesiology, 22(5), 768–776. doi:10.1016/j.jelekin.2012.02.012

Here is how you can run further exams from home, based upon the work of the Carrick Institute of Neuroscience and Rehabilitation, Cape Canaveral, Florida, if you don't have a local neurologist.

Neurological examination to determine brain side to ADJUST.>>

	CEREBELLUM	
LEFT		**RIGHT**
Left finger to nose		Right finger to nose
Left past pointing		Right past pointing
Left supination/pronation		Right supination/pronation
Left piano		Right piano
Decrease eye UL, DR, over left		Decrease eye UR, DL over right
Nystagmus spin target left		Nystagmus spin target right

	BRAIN	
LEFT		**RIGHT**
Left BP high		Right BP high
Lt distal myo weak.		Right distal myo weak.
Lt exotropia		Right exotropia
Left eye convergence off		Right eye convergence off
Left parietal arm drift		Right parietal arm drift
Left smell decreased		Right smell decreased
Left palatal paresis		Right palatal paresis
Left tongue pointing		Right tongue pointing
Decreased OPK Lt		Decreased right OPK*

ie: since left cerebellum goes to right brain, we treat left C0–C1.

*https://www.youtube.com/watch?v=D9dP02kd1Qk   Shows how OPK works.

https://www.youtube.com/watch?v=2juOEODwjJs   OPK to right

https://www.youtube.com/watch?v=2IPNw–mjbW8   OPK to the left (From my good friend Dr Davis.)

Home treatments:

Left brain friendly smells   Rt brain bad smells

Left Lt sudoku, crosswords   Rt Mazes, word search

Friendly faces and memories   New images and crazy art–music

Tap left foot	Tap right foot
Tap Lt hand to flashes of light	Rt Hand tapping to light
Spin in a chair to the left	Read nouns aloud
Vibration to left mastoid	Vibration Rt mastoid
Trace a maze	

The trick is that the frontal lobe processes info from opposite cerebellum 95% of time.

Eye movement up to weak cerebellar side and down to contralateral foot.

The left temporal lobe likes visual landmarks, and doing word lists, and music into the RIGHT ear, and pleasant smells up left nostril.

The right temporal lobe likes music into left ear, and bad smells up right nostril.

So there you have it, more ways than you thought possible to help yourself or your loved one.

A special thanks to my friend Dr. Adam Davis DC, DIBAK, DABCA, DCBCN, DACNB

This book is conceived by Dr. John W. Jung MS DC FIAMA FACMUAP

He can be reached at **jungjohn5@gmail.com** for more information or speaking engagements.